The Usborne
First
Encyclopedia
of
Our World

Felicity Brooks

Illustrated by David Hancock

Designed by Susannah Owen

Geography consultant: John Davidson
Managing designer: Mary Cartwright
Design development: Rachel Wells
Digital artwork: Michèle Busby and Nicola Butler
Picture researcher: Ruth King
Editorial development: Kamini Khanduri
Assistant editor: Rosie Heywood

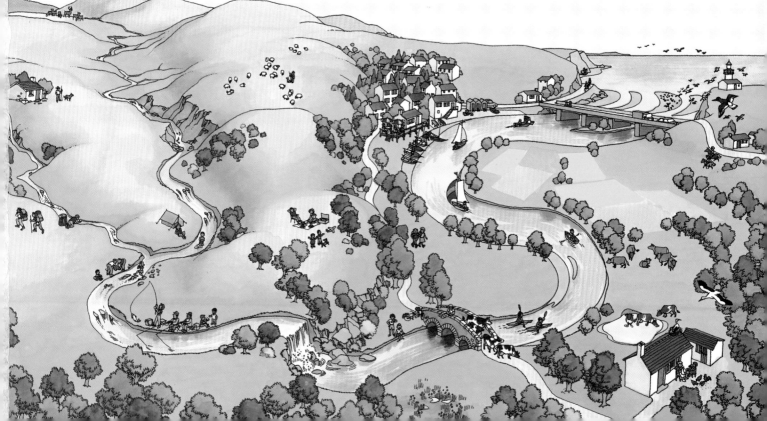

Using Internet links

There are lots of exciting places on the Internet where you can find out about the geography of our world. This book contains descriptions of Web sites that you can visit by clicking on links on the Usborne Quicklinks Web site. Just go to **www.usborne-quicklinks.com** and enter the keywords "our world". Here are some of the things you can do on the sites described in this book:

- Do a quiz about the Earth's atmosphere
- Build your own virtual satellite
- Watch short movies of some desert animals
- Take a virtual tour underground

Safety on the Internet

Here are a few simple rules to help keep you safe while you are online:

- Ask your parent's or guardian's permission before you connect to the Internet.
- Never give out information about yourself, such as your real name, address or phone number.
- Never arrange to meet someone you started talking to on the Internet.
- If a site asks you to log in or register by typing your name or e-mail address, ask permission from an adult first.
- If you receive an e-mail from someone you don't know, tell an adult. Don't reply to it.

Downloadable pictures

Pictures in this book that have the ★ symbol next to them can be downloaded from Usborne Quicklinks and printed out free of charge, for use in homework or projects. The pictures must not be copied or distributed for any commercial purpose. To find the pictures, go to **www.usborne-quicklinks.com** and follow the simple instructions there.

Site availability

The links in Usborne Quicklinks are regularly updated, but occasionally, you may get a message that a site is unavailable. This might be temporary, so try again later. If any of the sites close down, we will, if possible, replace them with alternatives. You will find an up-to-date list of sites in Usborne Quicklinks.

What you need

Most of the Web sites listed in this book can be accessed using a standard home computer and a Web browser (the software that lets you look at information from the Internet). Some sites need extra programs (plug-ins) to play sound or show videos or animations. If you go to a site and do not have the necessary plug-in, a message will come up on the screen. There is usually a button on the site that you can click on to download the plug-in. Alternatively, go to Usborne Quicklinks and click on **Net Help**. There, you can find links to download plug-ins.

Notes for parents

The Web sites described in this book are regularly reviewed and the links in Usborne Quicklinks are updated. However, the content of a Web site may change at any time and Usborne Publishing is not responsible for the content on any Web site other than its own. We recommend that children are supervised while on the Internet, that they do not use Internet Chat Rooms, and that you use Internet filtering software to block unsuitable material. Please ensure that your children read and follow the safety guidelines printed on the left. For more information, see the "Net Help" area on the Usborne Quicklinks Web site.

A COMPUTER IS NOT ESSENTIAL TO USE THIS BOOK

This book is a complete, superb, self-contained information book by itself.

Contents

Our planet

Our planet is called the Earth. It's the only planet where we know people, plants and animals live. There are lots of countries on the Earth. What's the name of yours?

This is a house...

in a town...

in a country...

on planet Earth.

If you went up in a spacecraft and looked at the Earth, this is what you'd see.

Swirling white clouds

Blue seas and oceans

Brown and green land

4

The atmosphere

The Earth is protected by a blanket of gases, called the atmosphere. It stretches from the surface of the Earth over 900km (560 miles) into space. The sky you can see is part of the atmosphere.

Earth

The atmosphere

The atmosphere helps to keep you warm at night.

In the daytime, it helps to protect you from the Sun's heat and light.

What's inside the Earth?

The Earth is made of rock and metal. If you could cut it in half, you would see different layers inside.

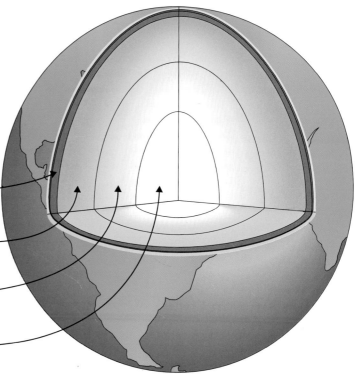

First, there's solid rock...

then hot, sticky rock which moves...

then very hot, soft metal.

In the middle, there's solid metal.

Go to **www.usborne-quicklinks.com** for a link to a Web site where you can try a quiz about the Earth's atmosphere.

What's out in space?

It's hard to imagine how big space is. There are billions of stars, planets and moons in it. Some are so far away, it would take millions of years to reach them.

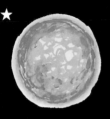

A star is a huge ball of hot gas.

A planet goes around a star.

A moon goes around a planet.

The Solar System

In our part of space, there are nine planets going around a star called the Sun. Together, they are known as the Solar System.

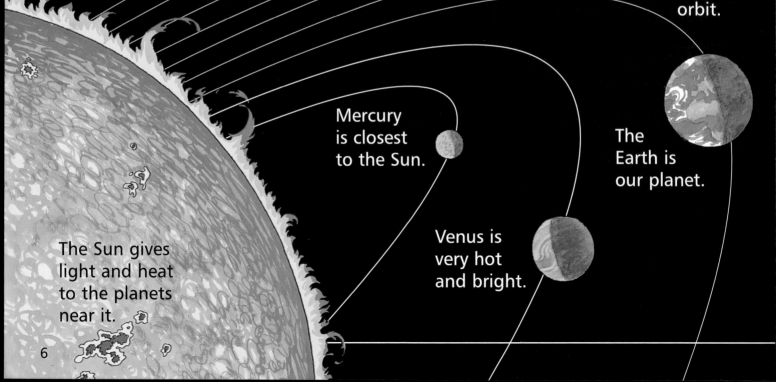

A planet's path is called its orbit.

Mercury is closest to the Sun.

The Earth is our planet.

Venus is very hot and bright.

The Sun gives light and heat to the planets near it.

Go to **www.usborne-quicklinks.com** for a link a Web site where you can find fun facts about the planets and play space games.

Looking at space

If you look up at the sky at night, you can see the Moon, lots of stars and some of the planets.

Stars look tiny because they are so far away.

People use telescopes to see more clearly.

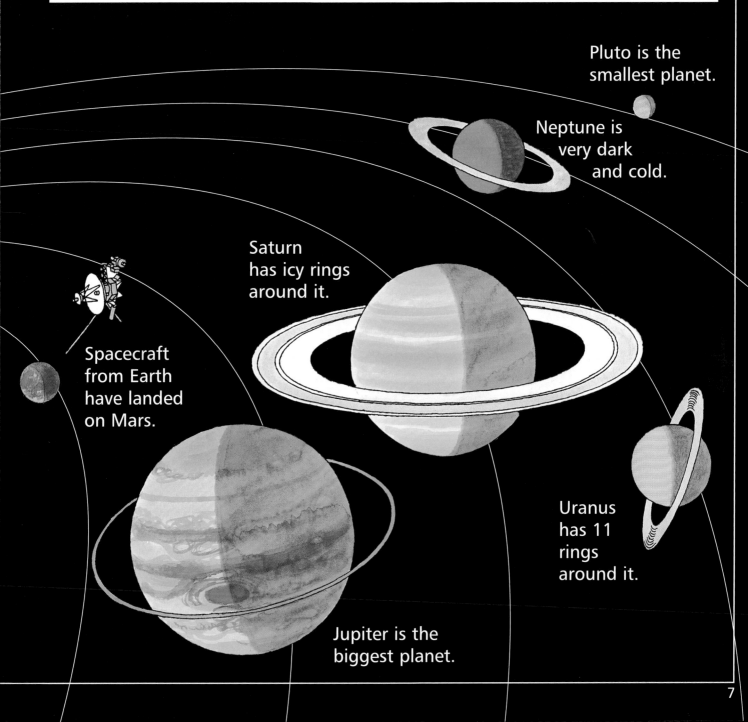

Pluto is the smallest planet.

Neptune is very dark and cold.

Saturn has icy rings around it.

Spacecraft from Earth have landed on Mars.

Uranus has 11 rings around it.

Jupiter is the biggest planet.

On the Moon

The Moon has no air and nobody lives there, but people have visited it six times. It took three days to get there in a spacecraft.

Radio antenna

Helmet

Plastic visor

Tanks of air for astronaut to breathe

People who explore space are called astronauts. They have to wear spacesuits to survive outside their spacecraft.

Control pack

Pocket for rocks

This astronaut is collecting rocks to bring back to Earth.

There's no wind or rain to sweep away footprints. How many can you see?

Going to the Moon

The astronauts went to the Moon in a rocket. They were inside the command capsule at the very top.

Five engines blast the rocket away from the Earth.

Command capsule

Stage 2 engines start up.

Stage 1 drops off when its fuel runs out.

Stage 2 drops off.

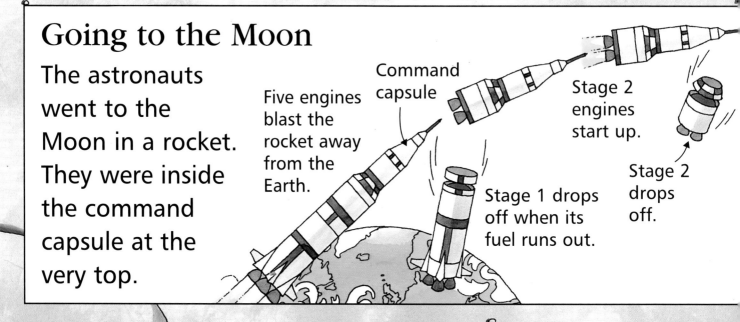

Moon mountain

The astronauts landed in a spacecraft called a lunar module.

The astronauts can drive around in this Lunar Roving Vehicle.

The Moon is covered in rocks, dust and craters.

Crater

Craters are made by huge lumps of rock called meteorites that crash into the Moon.

Saturn 5

Command capsule

Lunar module inside here

Stage 3

Stage 2

Stage 1

The Saturn 5 rocket took the first people to the Moon.

Stage 3 engines start up.

Tip drops off.

The capsule unlinks and turns around. It locks onto the lunar module and pulls it out. The astronauts crawl into the module.

The module lands on the Moon. The capsule flies around it. The module returns to the capsule when the astronauts are ready to go home.

Stage 3 drops off.

Go to **www.usborne-quicklinks.com** for a link to an interesting Web site where you can find out about the first men on the Moon.

Landsat
satellite

Looking at the Earth

Out in space there are spacecraft called satellites and space stations. They take pictures of the Earth which help us to learn about our planet.

Satellite pictures

Satellites fly around and around the Earth. There's no one in them, but they can send back information.

Scientists turn this into pictures that help them see how hot the Earth is, or what the weather will be like.

This satellite picture shows a hurricane (a big storm) about to hit the USA.

This shows the city of Washington DC, USA. The Potomac River is blue.

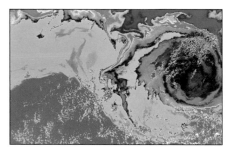

This shows the different temperatures of the sea. The hottest part is red.

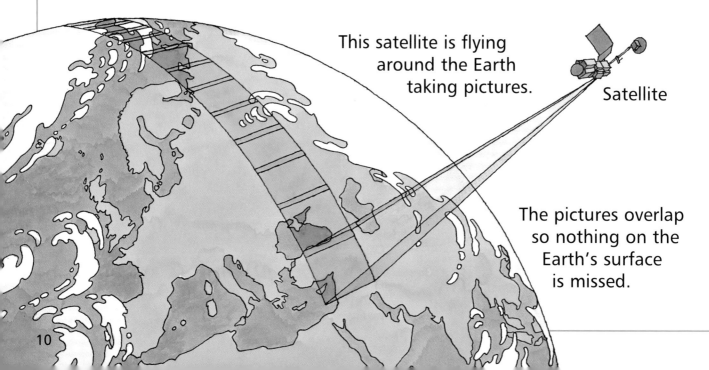

This satellite is flying around the Earth taking pictures.

Satellite

The pictures overlap so nothing on the Earth's surface is missed.

Space stations

Space stations go around the Earth about 400km (250 miles) up. People live and work on them. They take pictures of the Earth and other planets and stars.

Up to 6 astronauts live in this space station. How many can you see here?

★

These big wings are solar panels. They can make electricity from sunlight.

This astronaut is working at the control station.

In space, everything is weightless, so people float around.

The space shuttle

The space shuttle is like a plane that can travel into space. It blasts off like a rocket and glides back after a few weeks.

Fuel tank

Rocket booster

When the shuttle lifts off it has a fuel tank and 2 rocket boosters. They drop off soon after.

USA

United States

NASA
Challenger

Shuttle

Main engines

The shuttle takes people to space stations and puts satellites into space. Up to 7 people can live in it.

11

Day and night

When it is day for you, it is night for people on the other side of the world. When it's their day, it's your night.

The Sun's light can't reach this side of the Earth, so it's night here.

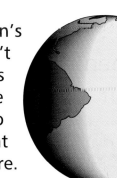

The Sun is shining on this side of the Earth, so it's day here.

Sunrise and sunset

The Sun rises in the morning when your side of the Earth turns to face the Sun.

The Sun sets in the evening when your side of the Earth turns away from the Sun.

Turning Earth

Day changes to night, and night to day, because the Earth turns. As it turns, different parts face the Sun.

This part of the Earth is facing the Sun, so it's day in the USA.

A few hours later, the USA has turned away from the Sun, so it's night there now.

The Earth keeps turning all the time.

After 24 hours, it has turned all the way around, so now it's day again in the USA.

Moon in the way

The only time it's dark in the day is when the Moon blocks out the Sun. This is called a total eclipse of the Sun. A total eclipse doesn't happen very often and it only lasts a few minutes.

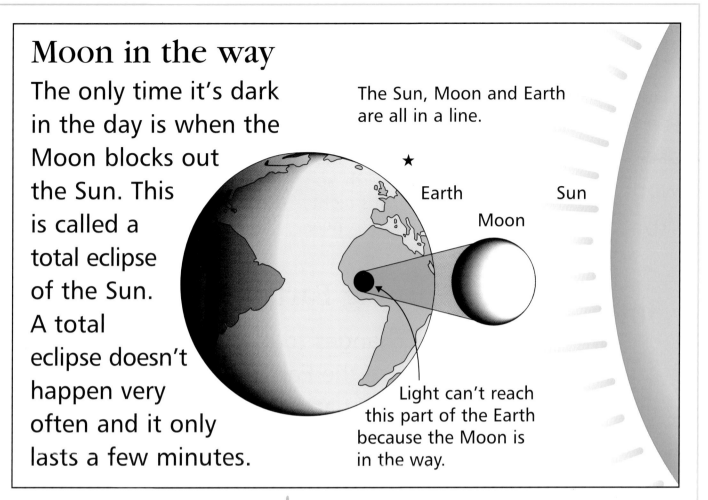

The Sun, Moon and Earth are all in a line.

★

Earth

Sun

Moon

Light can't reach this part of the Earth because the Moon is in the way.

Making shadows

On a sunny day, you stop some sunlight from reaching the ground. This is what makes your shadow.

Shadows point away from the Sun.

Cloudy days

Even on a cloudy day the Sun is shining on your part of the Earth. You just can't see it because the clouds hide it.

The seasons

Spring, summer, autumn and winter are the four seasons. The weather changes from season to season because of the way the Earth travels around the Sun.

The weather starts to get warm in spring.

The coldest season is winter. Nights are long. Days are short.

It's hot in summer. Nights are short and days are long.

After summer comes autumn. It starts to get cold again.

Earth words

Here are some words which are helpful when you want to know how the seasons work.

The poles are at the top and bottom of the Earth.

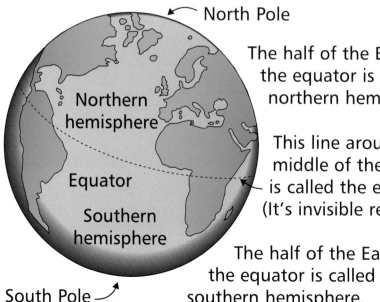

North Pole

The half of the Earth above the equator is called the northern hemisphere.

Northern hemisphere

This line around the middle of the Earth is called the equator. (It's invisible really.)

Equator

Southern hemisphere

The half of the Earth below the equator is called the southern hemisphere.

South Pole

Why the seasons change

The Earth is not upright as it goes around the Sun. It is tilted a little to one side. This means that during the year, first one half and then the other is nearer the Sun and gets more sunlight. This makes the seasons change.

Neither hemisphere is tilted towards the Sun in March. It's spring in the north, autumn in the south.

In December and January the southern hemisphere is tilted towards the Sun, so it's summer there.

It's winter in the northern hemisphere in December, because that half is tilted away from the Sun.

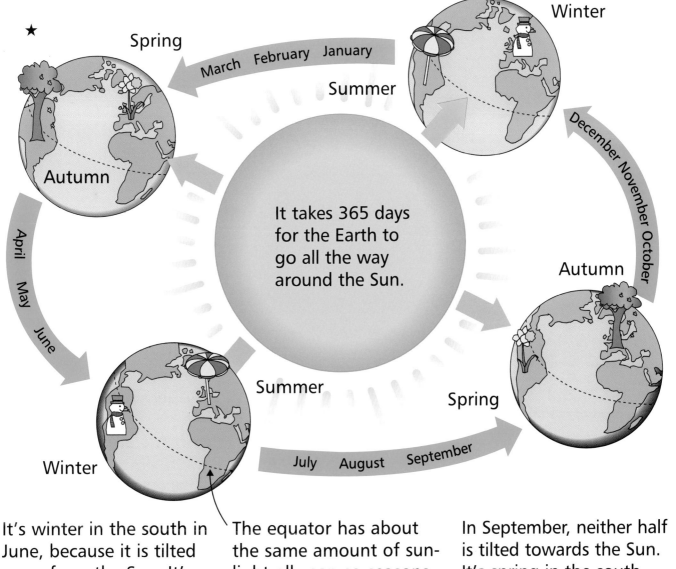

Spring

★

March February January

Summer

Winter

December November October

Autumn

It takes 365 days for the Earth to go all the way around the Sun.

April May June

Autumn

Spring

Summer

July August September

Winter

It's winter in the south in June, because it is tilted away from the Sun. It's summer in the north.

The equator has about the same amount of sunlight all year, so seasons change very little there.

In September, neither half is tilted towards the Sun. It's spring in the south and autumn in the north.

The weather

There are lots of different kinds of weather. It can be sunny, windy, rainy or snowy.

The three main things that make the weather happen are the Sun, the air and water.

The Sun gives heat to the Earth.

The air moves to make wind around us.

Water makes snow, rain and clouds.

The same rain

There isn't any new water on the Earth. The same rain falls again and again. Follow the numbers to see what happens.

3 The drops get bigger and join together into clouds.

2 Tiny, invisible drops of water rise up into the air.

4 When the drops get too heavy, they fall as raindrops.

1 The Sun heats up the water in rivers and seas.

5 Rivers run back into the sea.

What is snow?

Snowflakes fall instead of raindrops when it is very cold. They are made of tiny pieces of ice.

Every snowflake is different, but they all have 6 points.

Rainbows

You see a rainbow when the Sun shines through tiny drops of water in the air after it has rained. The sunlight divides into...

red
orange
yellow
green
blue
indigo
violet

Cloud clues

Clouds can give us clues about the weather.

Little, white, fluffy clouds mean good weather in summer.

Wispy clouds high in the sky show rain and wind may be coming.

Very tall, dark, fluffy clouds may bring thunderstorms.

Storms and winds

In a big storm, the wind blows very hard. There's usually lots of rain or snow. There may be thunder and lightning too. This picture shows what can happen near the sea when there's a very big storm.

Fallen trees block roads.

The wind blows tiles off roofs.

Chimneys sometimes break off.

Hats fly off.

More storms

★ A tornado is a spinning funnel of wind. It whirls along sucking up anything in its path.

★ Lightning is a big spark of electricity in the sky. Thunder is the noise that the spark makes.

★ A hurricane is a huge storm with lots of wind and rain. It can destroy towns and forests.

Trees bend and sway. Branches break off.

It's very hard to walk against the wind. You can't use an umbrella.

Waves smash into the land.

Flying objects may break windows.

Small rocks and pebbles are thrown onto the land.

How many buildings has this storm damaged?

Strong winds make enormous waves.

Boats are tossed around by the waves.

Rocks and fossils

There are lots of kinds of rocks. They are made in different ways. Some are made by heat from inside the Earth. Some are made when sand, mud and pieces of plants and animals are washed into rivers and seas.

Rocky layers

Sand, mud and pieces of plants and animals that sink and settle at the bottom of the sea are known as sediment.

Layers of sediment

Layers of sediment build up slowly. Over millions of years the bottom layers get squeezed and stuck together and become sedimentary rocks.

Fiery rocks

Sometimes hot, sticky rock from inside the Earth breaks through the surface.

Volcano

Hot, sticky rock

Hot, sticky rock pours out of a volcano. When it cools it becomes hard. This kind of rock is known as igneous rock. Igneous means "fiery".

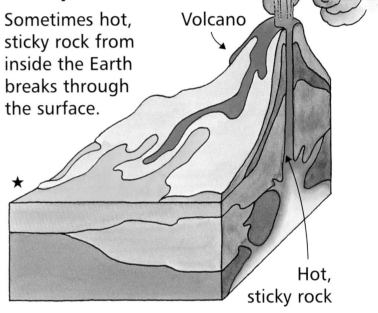

The Grand Canyon in Arizona, USA, is formed from layers of sedimentary rock.

Go to **www.usborne-quicklinks.com** for a link to a useful Web site where you can find out how to look for fossils.

Fossils

Fossils are the stony remains of animals that lived millions of years ago. Most fossils are found in sedimentary rock.

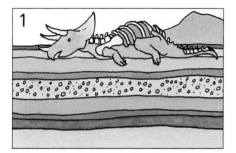

When an animal dies, its soft parts rot away but its bones are left. If they sink into a muddy place, they get covered in sediment.

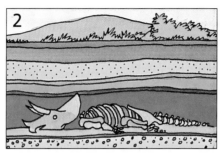

Over millions of years the layers of sediment slowly harden into rock. The rock keeps the shape of the animal's bones in it.

Millions of years later, people sometimes find fossil bones or shells inside rocks. They have to dig them up carefully.

Fossil of a sea animal called an ammonite

★ Trilobite fossil

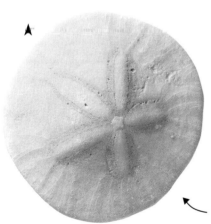

This is the fossil of a sea creature called a sand dollar which lived on the seabed.

The Colorado River made the Grand Canyon. It started to wear the rock away millions of years ago.

Earthquakes

An earthquake happens when huge rocks deep under the ground slip and push against each other. This makes the ground above shake. Big earthquakes like this one don't happen very often.

There's lots of smoke from fires.

Houses fall down.

Fires start when electricity cables or gas pipes break.

Trees are pulled out of the soil.

What happens in houses?

Hanging things swing in a small earthquake.

In a bigger one, some things fall to the floor.

In an even bigger one, the walls start to crack.

In a very big one, the whole house falls down.

Some specially made buildings stay standing.

Railway lines break.

The ground cracks open.

Cars slide off the road.

People try to run to safety.

Telephone lines fall down.

Staying safe

In countries with a lot of earthquakes, people learn ways of staying safe. Children have earthquake-safety lessons at school.

Indoors, it's safest to shelter under a table.

Outdoors, you're safest in a big open space.

Go to **www.usborne-quicklinks.com** for a link to an exciting Web site where you can watch animations of earthquakes.

23

Volcanoes

A volcano erupts when hot, sticky rock from inside the Earth bursts through the surface. The hot rock, called lava, pours down the sides of the volcano and over the land.

Huge clouds of ash and gas may billow up into the air.

"Bombs" of rock shoot up into the sky. Some are the size of buses.

Lava destroys everything it touches.

River of red-hot lava

Sea volcanoes

There are volcanoes under the sea. When one gets tall enough to appear above the waves, it makes an island.

The hole at the top of a volcano is called a crater.

Layers of ash and lava

Lava often moves quite slowly, so people usually have time to move away before it harms them.

Alive, asleep or dead?

A volcano may be active (alive), dormant (asleep) or extinct (dead).

★

A volcano that erupts quite often is called an active volcano.

★

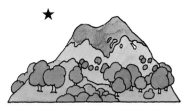

A dormant volcano hasn't erupted for a long time, but may again in the future.

★

An extinct volcano hasn't erupted for at least 100,000 years. Some towns are built on extinct volcanoes.

Go to www.usborne-quicklinks.com for a link to a Web site where you can look at some amazing pictures of volcanoes.

Following a river

A river starts high up in hills or mountains. The water comes from rain or melted snow. It flows downhill until it reaches the sea. Follow this river to see how it changes.

1 The beginning of a river is called its source.

2 Lots of streams may join together to make a river.

3 The water wears the rock away to make a valley shaped like a V.

4 Other smaller rivers called tributaries may join the river and make it bigger.

The sides of the river are called riverbanks.

People sometimes put big, flat stepping stones in a river. You can step on them to cross it.

These fishermen are trying to catch fish that live in the river.

5 Here the river flows fast over rocks and stones.

This is a waterfall. The water flows very fast here.

Waterfalls

A waterfall forms where a river flows from hard rock to soft rock. The water wears the soft rock away faster than the hard rock. This makes a big step.

10 The place where a river joins the sea is called the mouth of the river.

Lots of birds feed on the little animals that live in the sand.

Bank of sand

8 The river carries lots of sand and mud to the sea.

9 The river drops most of its sand and mud when it reaches the sea.

6 Here the river starts to flow in big loops called meanders.

7 The river is deeper and wider here.

You can cross a river on a bridge.

Floods

A flood is when water covers land that is usually dry. It may happen when there is a lot of rain in a short time, or when it pours with rain for a long time. Rivers get too full and spill onto the land.

People being rescued by boat

As the water rises, animals and people try to stay safe on roofs.

More floods

A flash flood is a sudden rush of water. It happens when a lot of rain falls in one place in a short time.

Huge waves can cause floods. They are made by storms or by undersea volcanoes or earthquakes.

Some floods happen when snow and ice melt. The soil is still frozen so water cannot soak into it.

Go to **www.usborne-quicklinks.com** for a link to a Web site where you can find out about floods and try some fun puzzles.

Not all the rain can seep into the ground, so it covers the land.

These people are trying to stop the water. They are making a wall of bags filled with sand.

Monsoon floods

The monsoon is a wind. In Asia, it blows one way all summer and the other way all winter. In summer it brings very heavy rain from the oceans.

The monsoon rain often floods cities and homes but people try to carry on with their lives as normal.

Farmers need the monsoon rain for their crops to grow. Plants such as rice grow well in the wet soil.

In the mountains

As you climb up a mountain, it gets colder and colder. Some mountains have snow on the top all the year around.

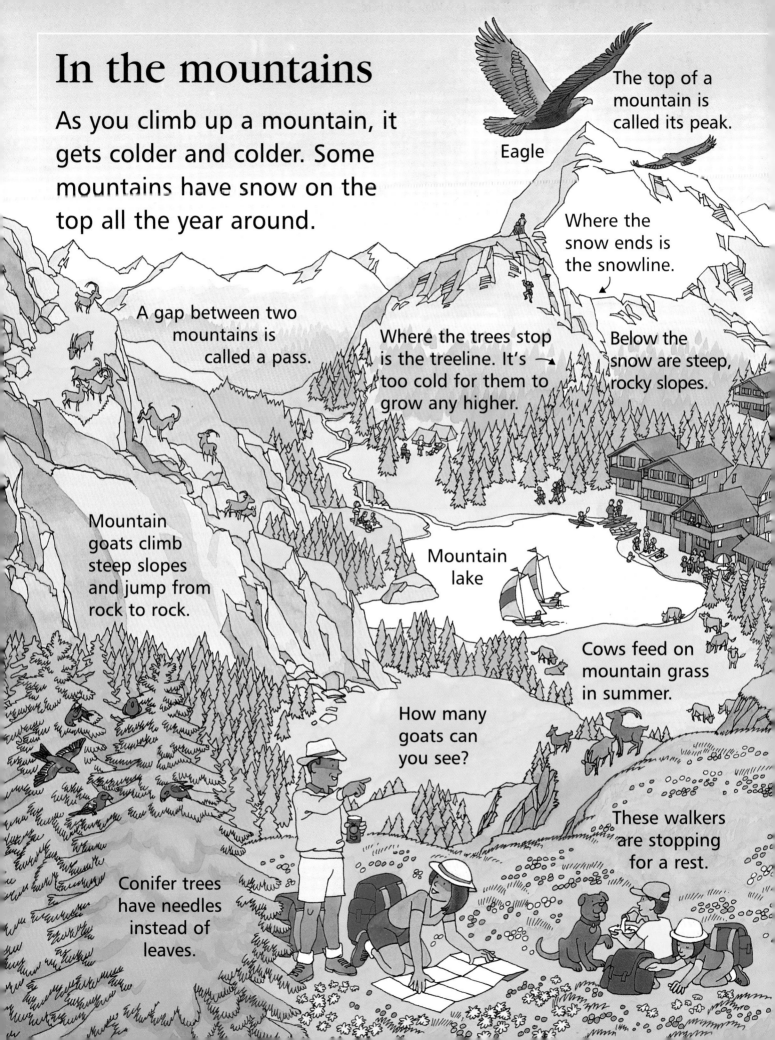

Eagle

The top of a mountain is called its peak.

Where the snow ends is the snowline.

A gap between two mountains is called a pass.

Where the trees stop is the treeline. It's too cold for them to grow any higher.

Below the snow are steep, rocky slopes.

Mountain goats climb steep slopes and jump from rock to rock.

Mountain lake

Cows feed on mountain grass in summer.

How many goats can you see?

These walkers are stopping for a rest.

Conifer trees have needles instead of leaves.

Winter fun

In the winter the mountains are covered in snow. It's very cold, but fun for sports.

This helicopter rescues people who hurt themselves in the mountains.

Cable cars carry people up to the ski slopes.

A row of mountains is called a mountain range.

A chairlift takes skiers right to the top of the slope.

Skiers zigzag down the ski slopes.

Skating on a frozen lake

Avalanche!

An avalanche begins when a huge slab of snow starts to slide down a mountain.

The avalanche crashes downhill. It can knock over cars and bury everything in its way.

Rescue dogs sniff the snow. They can smell people who are buried and help dig them out.

The seashore

The seashore is where the sea meets the land. On most shores the sea moves up and down the beach. This is called the tide. At low tide a beach is dry. At high tide it's under water.

Cliff

Waves beat against cliffs and slowly wear them away.

Lifeboats help people in danger. Can you see why these people are in trouble?

When the wind blows over the sea it makes waves. They grow tall and topple over when they reach land.

Sand is made of tiny pieces of hard rock and seashells.

Headlands, cracks, caves and blowholes...

This headland is made of hard rock. The sea can't wear it away as fast as the rock around it.

Waves crashing onto the headland made this big crack. Little by little they will widen it into a cave.

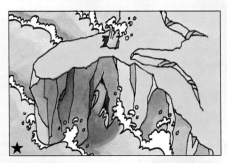

Waves have worn through the top of this cave and made a blowhole. Water spurts out at high tide.

Go to **www.usborne-quicklinks.com** for a link to a Web site where you can see how coasts change.

At night, a lighthouse shows ships where there are dangerous rocks or cliffs.

Boulders are big rocks which have fallen off the cliff.

Pebbles are bits of rock which the sea has worn smooth.

Pools of water are left among the rocks when the tide goes out. Lots of sea creatures live in them.

Seaweed

...arches, stacks and stumps

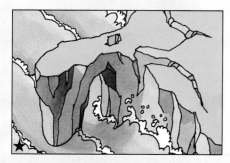

When waves wear away caves on both sides of a headland, the caves may meet and make an arch.

The waves keep pounding the arch until its top falls off. A pillar of rock called a stack is all that's left.

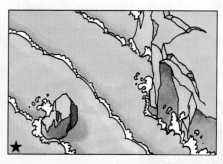

After many years all that is left of the stack is this stump. The rest has been worn away by the waves.

33

Seas and oceans

Seas and oceans cover almost three-quarters of the Earth. There are five oceans and lots of smaller areas of salty water, called seas, bays and gulfs.

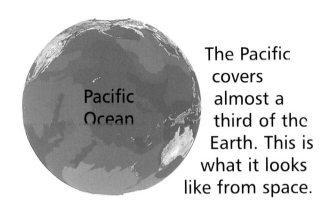

Pacific Ocean

The Pacific covers almost a third of the Earth. This is what it looks like from space.

This map of the world shows the oceans.

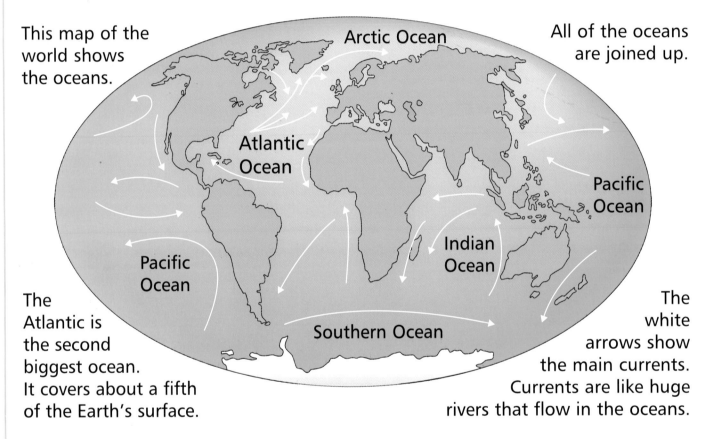

Arctic Ocean

Atlantic Ocean

Pacific Ocean

Indian Ocean

Pacific Ocean

Southern Ocean

All of the oceans are joined up.

The Atlantic is the second biggest ocean. It covers about a fifth of the Earth's surface.

The white arrows show the main currents. Currents are like huge rivers that flow in the oceans.

Catching fish

There are many ways of catching sea fish. This boy is using a fishing rod.

This boat drags this net along to catch fish which live near the seabed.

These are called creels. They are used to catch crabs under the sea.

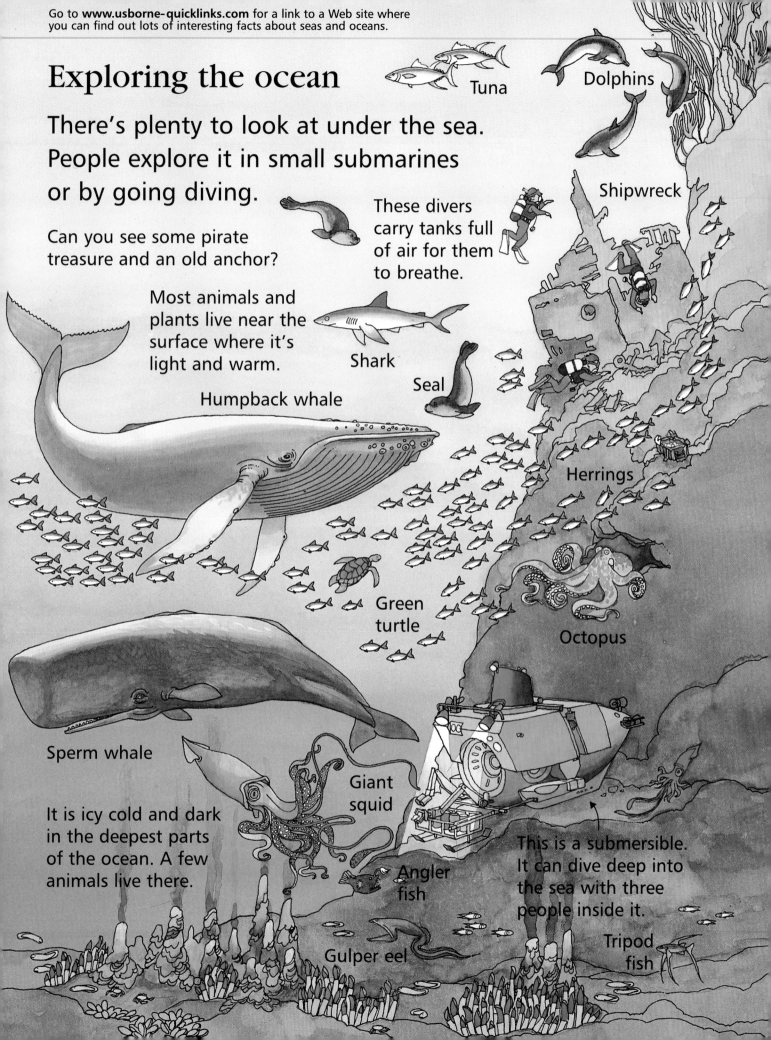

Go to **www.usborne-quicklinks.com** for a link to a Web site where you can find out lots of interesting facts about seas and oceans.

Exploring the ocean

There's plenty to look at under the sea. People explore it in small submarines or by going diving.

Tuna

Dolphins

Shipwreck

Can you see some pirate treasure and an old anchor?

These divers carry tanks full of air for them to breathe.

Most animals and plants live near the surface where it's light and warm.

Shark

Seal

Humpback whale

Herrings

Green turtle

Octopus

Sperm whale

Giant squid

It is icy cold and dark in the deepest parts of the ocean. A few animals live there.

Angler fish

This is a submersible. It can dive deep into the sea with three people inside it.

Gulper eel

Tripod fish

Under the sea

The bottom of the sea is called the seabed. Under the water there are plains, mountains, volcanoes and valleys.

This is the continental shelf. The sea is quite shallow here.

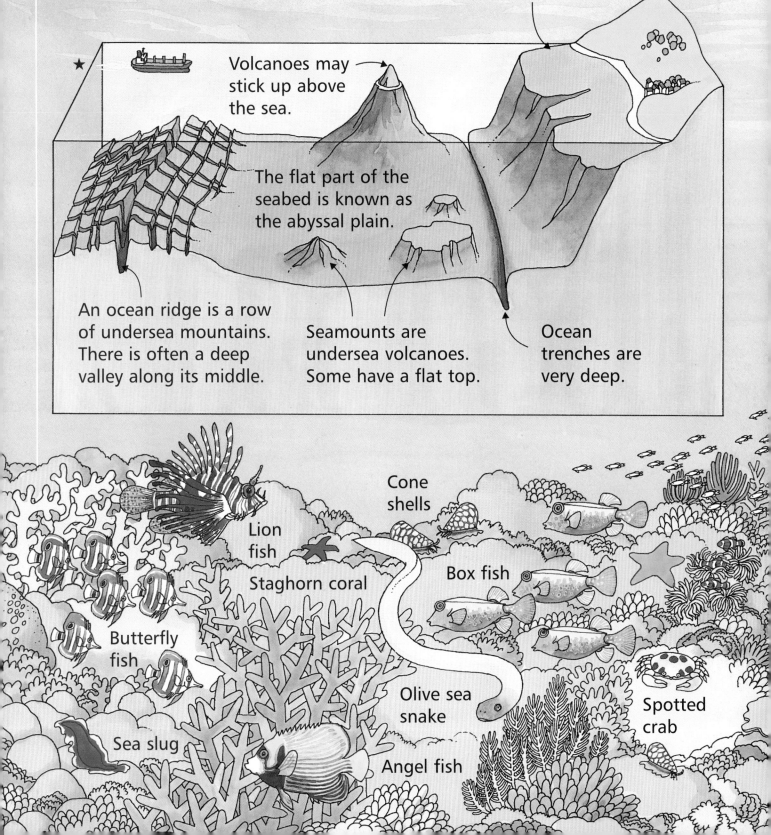

Volcanoes may stick up above the sea.

The flat part of the seabed is known as the abyssal plain.

An ocean ridge is a row of undersea mountains. There is often a deep valley along its middle.

Seamounts are undersea volcanoes. Some have a flat top.

Ocean trenches are very deep.

Lion fish

Cone shells

Box fish

Staghorn coral

Butterfly fish

Olive sea snake

Spotted crab

Sea slug

Angel fish

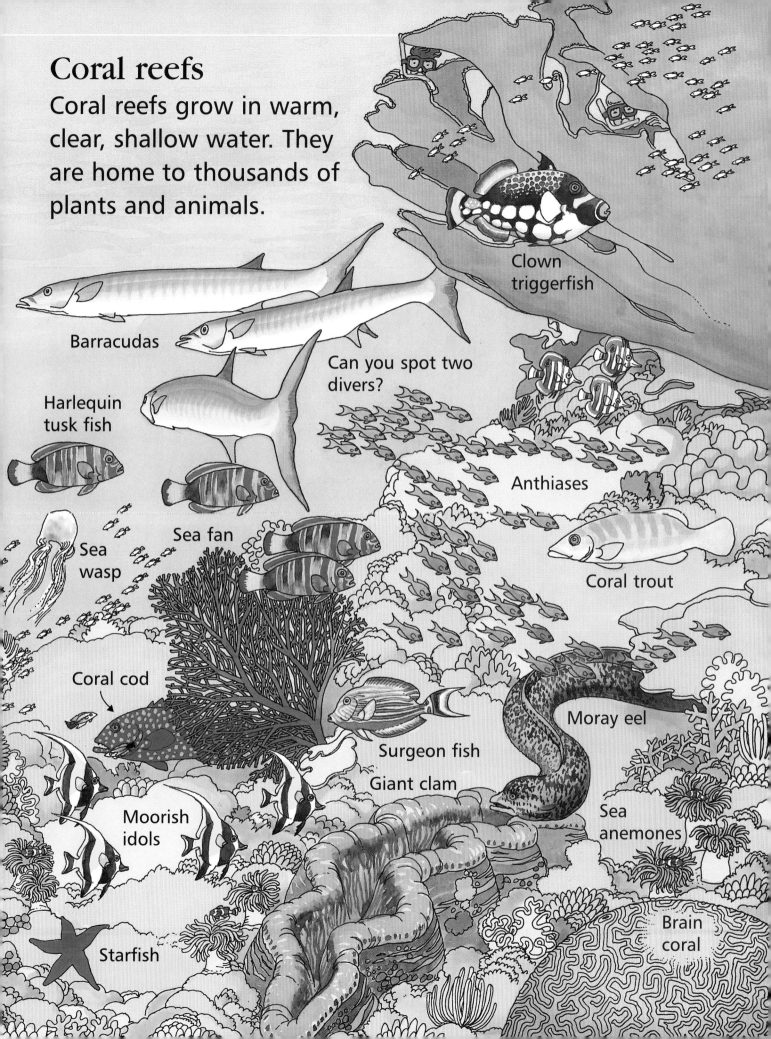

Coral reefs

Coral reefs grow in warm, clear, shallow water. They are home to thousands of plants and animals.

Clown triggerfish

Barracudas

Harlequin tusk fish

Can you spot two divers?

Anthiases

Sea wasp

Sea fan

Coral trout

Coral cod

Surgeon fish

Moray eel

Giant clam

Moorish idols

Sea anemones

Starfish

Brain coral

Under the ground

There's a world beneath your feet which you don't see. If you could look under the ground, here are some things you might spot.

Moles tunnel in the soil. They make molehills when they come up to the surface.

Soil near the surface is called topsoil.

Rabbits live in burrows.

Roots stop trees from falling over. They suck up water from the soil, along with other things the tree needs to grow.

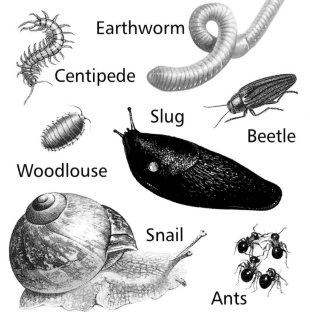

Little creatures

Many small creatures live in the topsoil. Here are some you might see.

Earthworm

Centipede

Slug

Beetle

Woodlouse

Snail

Ants

Ancient pot

There may be things buried in the soil that belonged to people long ago.

Under the thick layer of soil, there is solid rock.

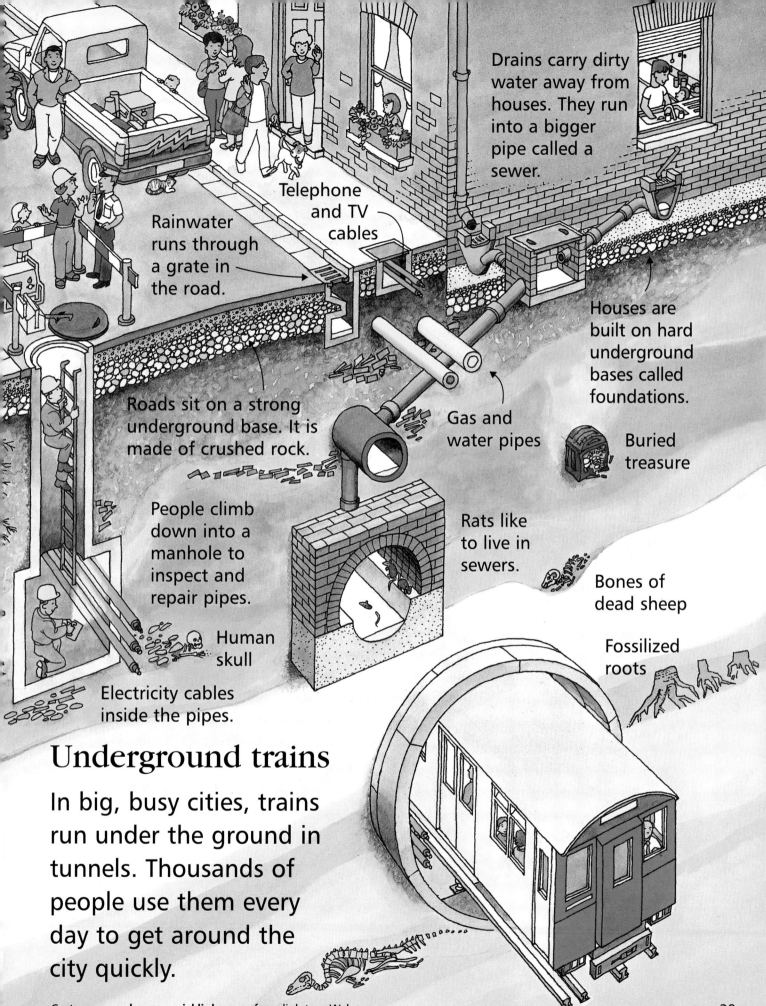

Drains carry dirty water away from houses. They run into a bigger pipe called a sewer.

Telephone and TV cables

Rainwater runs through a grate in the road.

Roads sit on a strong underground base. It is made of crushed rock.

Gas and water pipes

Houses are built on hard underground bases called foundations.

Buried treasure

People climb down into a manhole to inspect and repair pipes.

Human skull

Rats like to live in sewers.

Bones of dead sheep

Fossilized roots

Electricity cables inside the pipes.

Underground trains

In big, busy cities, trains run under the ground in tunnels. Thousands of people use them every day to get around the city quickly.

Go to www.usborne-quicklinks.com for a link to a Web site where you can take a virtual tour under the ground.

Caves and caverns

A cave or cavern is like an underground room with walls made of rock. Some caves are just below the surface. Others are very deep underground.

Caves are full of strange, rocky shapes which are made by dripping water with dissolved rock in it.

Stalactites hang from the roof.

Waterfall

Stalactites and stalagmites can grow together to make columns.

Water drips down from stalactites to make stalagmites.

How caves are made

Each time it rains, the rainwater seeps through cracks in the rock.

Over a long, long time the water dissolves the rock and wears it away.

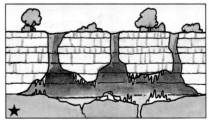

When the level of the water drops, empty caves and passages are left.

Go to **www.usborne-quicklinks.com** for a link to a Web site where you can read a story about caves.

Cavers

Cavers are people who explore caves for fun, or to find out more about them. They have special clothes and equipment.

Cavers often squeeze through narrow passages or wade through deep water to reach a cave.

Underground lake

Caver

Helmet with lamp

Strong rope for climbing down into cave

Thick overalls

Waterproof boots

Bears, bats and bison

Brown bears and black bears sleep through the long winter inside caves.

Horseshoe bat

Many kinds of bats spend the winter in caves. They fly out in the spring.

Painting of a bison

A long time ago, people lived in caves. They made pictures on the walls.

Dusty deserts

Deserts are the driest places in the world. Sometimes it doesn't rain for years and years. Most deserts are extremely hot in the day, but cool at night.

Sahara Desert

AFRICA

Deserts cover over a quarter of our planet. The biggest is the Sahara Desert in North Africa.

Desert homes have flat roofs, and small windows to keep the Sun out.

Palm trees

An oasis is a place where there is water and plants can grow.

Camels can last a week without water.

Euphorbia plant

How many antelopes can you spot?

Most deserts are rocky and bare. Only parts of them are covered in sand.

Sandgrouse

Jerboas hop along like miniature kangaroos.

Desert plants

Many desert plants have long roots, and stems which can soak up water.

Before rain ★

After rain ★

A barrel cactus swells with water when it rains.

★

A giant saguaro cactus may live for hundreds of years.

When the wind blows, the sand piles up into hills called sand dunes.

Lanner falcon

Desert people live in groups and move from place to place. They keep sheep, goats and camels.

Fennec foxes have huge ears which help them to lose heat.

Saw scaled adders slither along with an S-shaped wiggle.

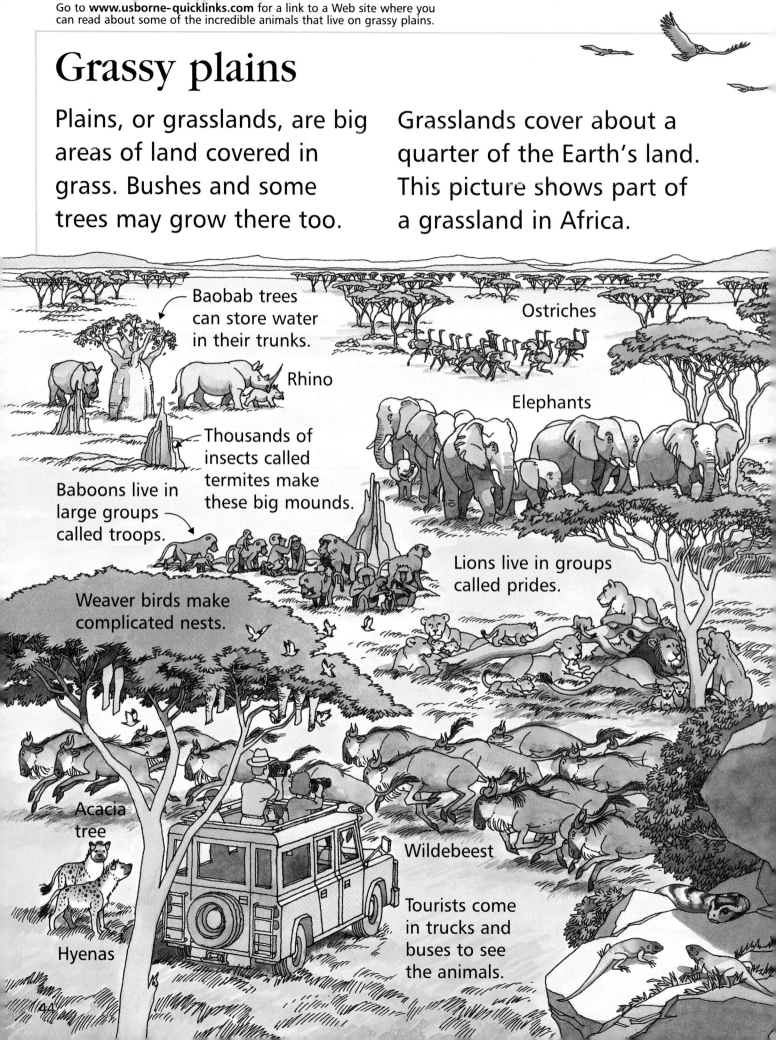

Go to **www.usborne-quicklinks.com** for a link to a Web site where you can read about some of the incredible animals that live on grassy plains.

Grassy plains

Plains, or grasslands, are big areas of land covered in grass. Bushes and some trees may grow there too.

Grasslands cover about a quarter of the Earth's land. This picture shows part of a grassland in Africa.

Baobab trees can store water in their trunks.

Ostriches

Rhino

Elephants

Thousands of insects called termites make these big mounds.

Baboons live in large groups called troops.

Lions live in groups called prides.

Weaver birds make complicated nests.

Acacia tree

Wildebeest

Tourists come in trucks and buses to see the animals.

Hyenas

44

Tourists in a hot air balloon

Vultures

The dry grass catches fire easily. It grows again when it rains.

Giraffes

Lots of animals come to a waterhole to drink and stay cool.

Antelopes

Warthog

Cheetahs

Zebras

Prairies

North American grasslands are called prairies. Most of them are now used as farmland.

This machine, called a combine harvester, is cutting wheat on a prairie farm in the USA.

In the rainforest

Thick, green rainforests grow in
hot, wet places near the equator.
It is warm all year there and it
rains nearly every day. Rainforests
are home to thousands of
different plants and animals.

Amazon
River

South
America

The biggest
rainforest is
the Amazon
Rainforest in
South America.
The Amazon
River runs
through it.

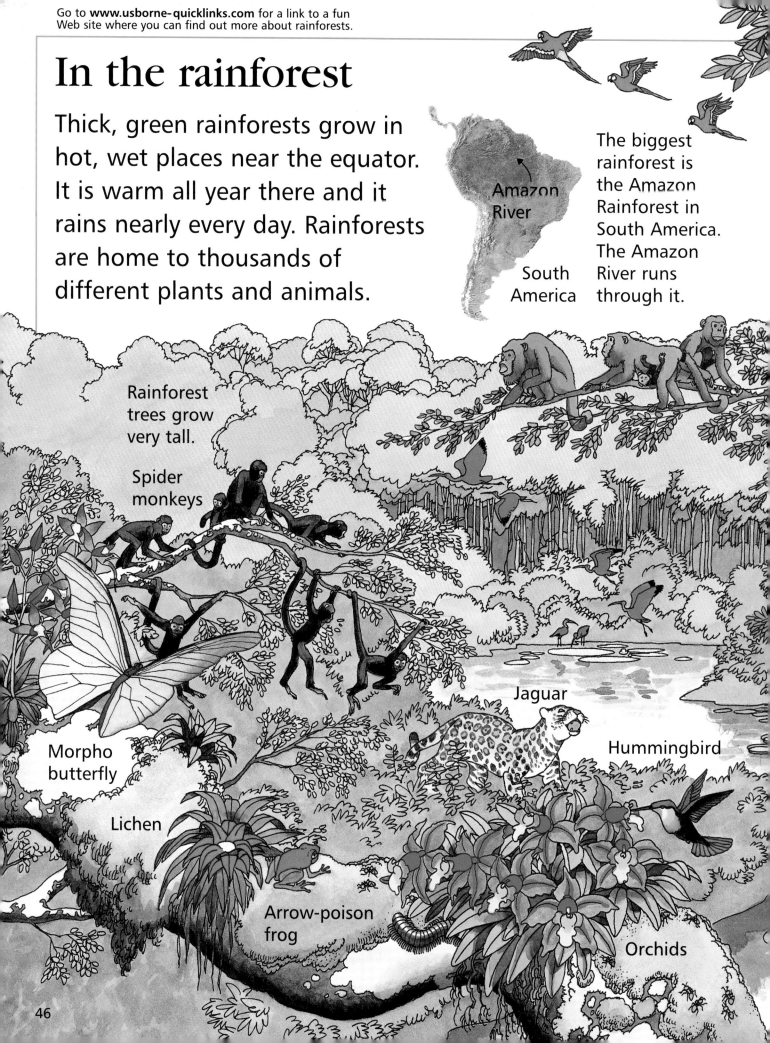

Rainforest
trees grow
very tall.

Spider
monkeys

Jaguar

Hummingbird

Morpho
butterfly

Lichen

Arrow-poison
frog

Orchids

Plants on trees

Many rainforest plants grow on the branches of trees where there is more light than on the ground.

Ferns

Scarlet macaws

Toucans

Bromeliad

Howler monkeys

Lianas are plants with long stems like ropes.

Sloths move very slowly.

Capybaras look like large guinea pigs.

Caiman

These big buttress roots hold the tall trees upright.

Giant armadillo

Scarlet ibis

Anacondas are huge snakes.

Matamata turtle

Giant water lily leaves

Icy world

This icy place near the South Pole is called the Antarctic. It's colder than anywhere else in the world. No one lives here all the time but people visit. There are lots of penguins. How many can you see?

Scientists studying the weather

Pointed iceberg

Flat-topped iceberg

Huge cliffs of ice

Tourists in a dinghy

Killer whale

Humpback whale

Seals

Scientists watching animals underwater

Fish

Go to **www.usborne-quicklinks.com** for a link to a Web site where you can take a virtual tour of Antarctica.

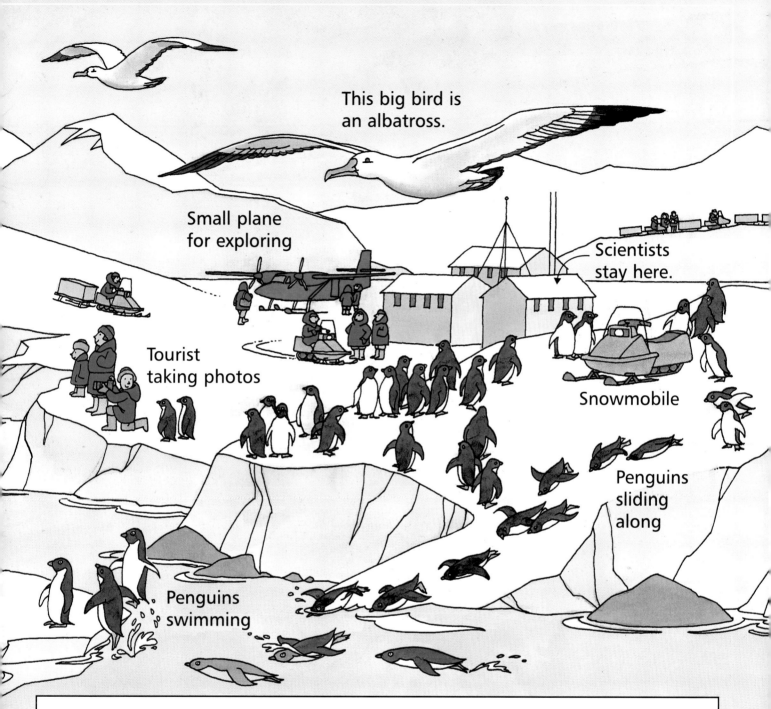

This big bird is an albatross.

Small plane for exploring

Scientists stay here.

Tourist taking photos

Snowmobile

Penguins sliding along

Penguins swimming

What is an iceberg?

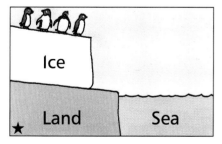

Ice

★ Land | Sea

A sheet of ice moves over the land to the sea.

★

At the sea, the ice moves out over the water.

★ Iceberg

A piece of ice breaks off. This is an iceberg.

Rivers of ice

Solid rivers of ice that move very slowly downhill are called glaciers. They are found in places where it is always very cold and shady. Glaciers are made from snow that falls at the top of a mountain and turns into ice.

Deep snow builds up in hollows high up in the mountains.

The top layers of snow press down on the bottom layers and turn them into solid ice.

The ice moves slowly down the mountain as more ice builds up behind it.

The glacier carries stones and pieces of rock down the mountain.

Other smaller glaciers may join the main one.

Deep cracks in the ice are called crevasses.

The glacier melts as it gets warmer farther down the mountain.

When glaciers melt

A long time ago there were far more glaciers than today. When they melted they left valleys which look like this.

Crevasses

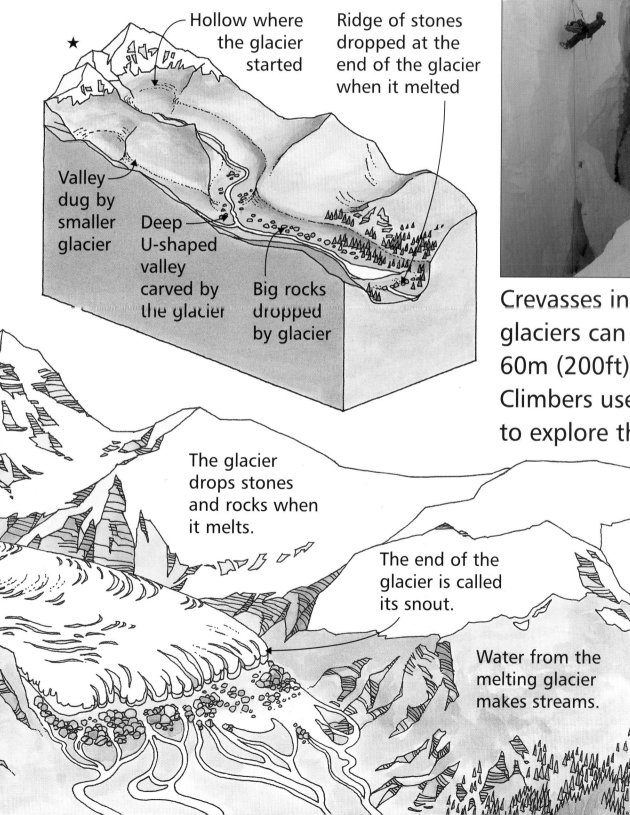

Hollow where the glacier started

Ridge of stones dropped at the end of the glacier when it melted

Valley dug by smaller glacier

Deep U-shaped valley carved by the glacier

Big rocks dropped by glacier

Crevasses in glaciers can be 60m (200ft) deep. Climbers use ropes to explore them.

The glacier drops stones and rocks when it melts.

The end of the glacier is called its snout.

Water from the melting glacier makes streams.

Go to **www.usborne-quicklinks.com** for a link to a Web site where you can compare three different cities.

In the city

A city is a big, busy town where many people live and work. There are lots of buildings and all kinds of jobs to be done. These are some of the things you might see in a city.

Offices

Apartments

School

Hotel

Taxi

Museum

Street cleaner

Road repairers

Police car

Hospital

Factories

Railway station

Bus

Mosque

Park

River

Shopping area

Window cleaners

Supermarket

Cities of the world

Venice, in Italy, has canals instead of roads. Everyone travels by boat.

New York, in the USA, has very tall buildings called skyscrapers.

Jaipur, in India, is known as the pink city, because it has so many pink buildings.

Useful Earth

We depend on the Earth to survive. It gives us food, air and water as well as all we need for building and making things. It also gives us the fuel we need for cooking, heating and making machines and engines go.

Sand is used to make glass.

Recycling

Used cans, bottles and paper can be collected and made into new things. This is called recycling. It makes less waste than throwing things away.

We eat many kinds of plants. Some are made into material, such as cotton, for clothes. Others are made into medicines.

Oil and natural gas come from under the ground or under the seabed. People drill for them from rigs.

You can put empty glass bottles in a bottle bank.

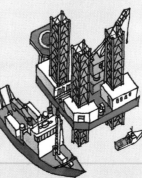
Oil and gas are used to make power. Oil can also be made into plastic, paint or glue.

Wood from trees can be
made into many things,
such as furniture and paper.

Animals give us
leather and wool
as well as milk,
meat and eggs.

Metal, coal, stone, clay and
other useful things are dug
out of the ground in places
called quarries or mines.

Fishing boats catch
fish from the sea.

Non-stop power

Oil, gas and coal may one
day run out. There are many
other ways of making power
from things that will
not run out, such as wind,
water and sunshine.

Wind turbines are giant
windmills. They can make
electricity from the wind.

Solar panels can soak up
heat from the Sun and
use it to make hot water.

Flowing water can drive
machines called turbines
that make electricity.

Go to **www.usborne-quicklinks.com** for a link to a Web site where you can
click on different parts of a house to find out how energy can be saved there.

The web of life

Plants, animals and people depend on other living things to survive. Animals and people eat plants, and some animals and people eat other animals. A food chain shows how plants and animals are connected.

Grass grows in the soil.

Hares eat grass.

Foxes eat hares.

Food webs

A food web is made of lots of food chains. It shows who eats who. Here's part of a food web in the Arctic.

Arctic fox

Wolf

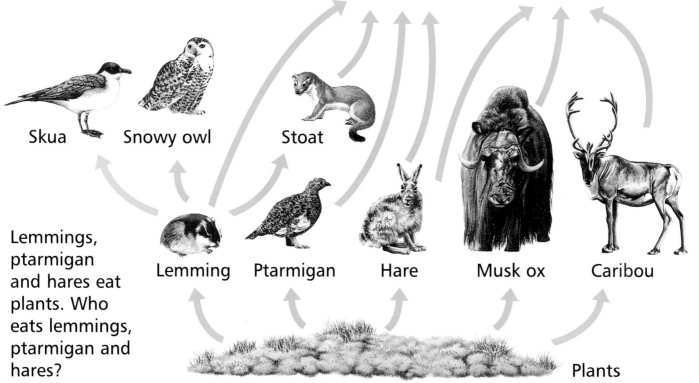

Skua   Snowy owl   Stoat

Lemmings, ptarmigan and hares eat plants. Who eats lemmings, ptarmigan and hares?

Lemming   Ptarmigan   Hare   Musk ox   Caribou

Plants

Sharing food

Different animals can live together in one place, even if they all eat plants. There's enough food to go around because they eat in different ways. This is how some grassland animals share plants.

Giraffes use their long necks to feed on leaves and twigs from the tops of trees.

Male giraffes stretch up to eat.

Elephants stretch up with their trunks to grab leaves and twigs, or down to pull up grass.

Female giraffes eat leaves by their mouths.

Gerenuks can stand on their back legs to eat the top leaves of bushes.

Warthogs feed on grass or dig up roots to eat.

Dik-diks eat the lowest part of bushes.

Black rhinos munch on leaves from bushes at the same level as their heads.

57

World in danger

There are many things that we do to our world which put animals, plants and people in danger.

Pollution

Litter, smoke from factories and cars, and oil that spills from ships at sea are all kinds of pollution. Pollution harms animals and people and the places where they live.

Smoke and fumes from factories and cars pollute the air.

Chemicals from factories and farms can get into the water and soil.

Litter looks horrible and can be dangerous.

Animals in danger

These animals are all endangered. This means that there are very few of them left and they could easily die out. This has happened because we have hunted them or destroyed the places where they live.

Tigers are endangered because people hunted them for their skins.

Golden lion tamarins became endangered when rainforests were cut down.

Rhinoceroses are killed for their horns, although this is against the law.

Fish, birds and other animals cannot live in polluted water.

Safe places

One way to help animals in danger is to set aside land where they can live safely. These places are called protected areas.

Grizzly bears live in the Yellowstone National Park, a protected area in the USA.

World map

This map shows the world's seas and oceans, its seven continents, climates and biggest cities. Do you know where you live on this map?

World climates

Climate is the usual kind of weather an area has. The different shaded areas on this map show these different climates:

■	Mountains -	cold for much of the year
▢	Polar climate -	very cold all year
■	Temperate climate -	some rain in all seasons
▢	Warm climate -	summers are hot and dry, winters are mild and wet
▢	Desert climate -	hot and very dry all year
■	Tropical climate -	hot all year, with heavy rain in the wet season
■	Equatorial climate -	hot and wet with rain every day

NORTH AMERICA

Atlantic Ocean

SOUTH AMERICA

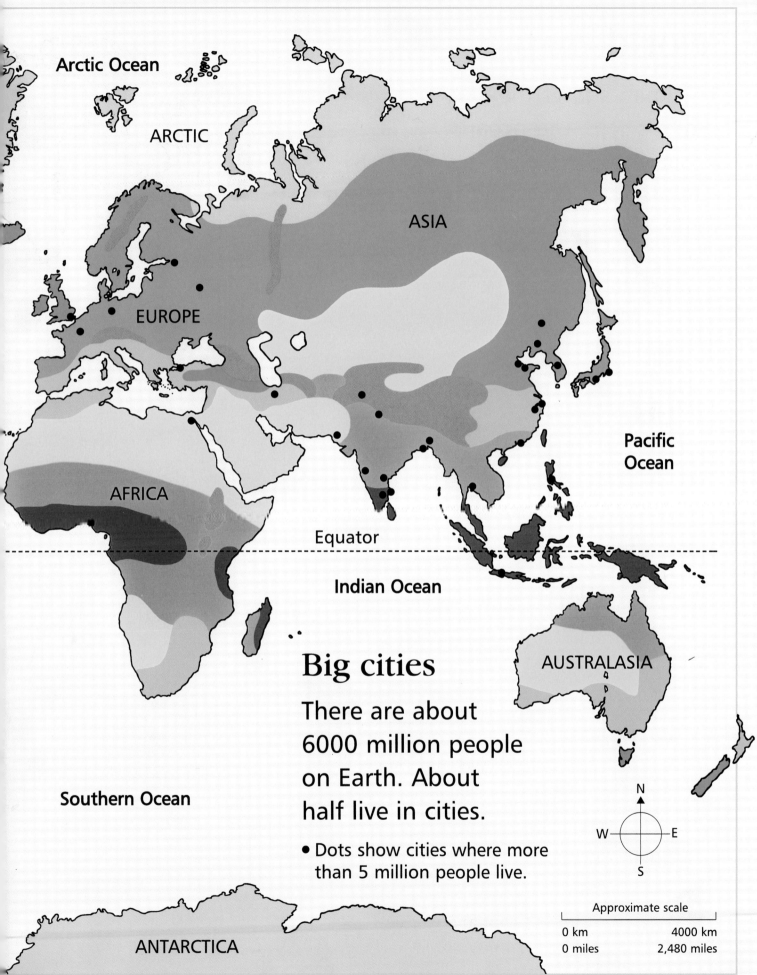

Arctic Ocean

ARCTIC

ASIA

EUROPE

Pacific
Ocean

AFRICA

Equator

Indian Ocean

Big cities

There are about
6000 million people
on Earth. About
half live in cities.

AUSTRALASIA

Southern Ocean

- Dots show cities where more
  than 5 million people live.

N

W—E

S

Approximate scale

0 km   4000 km
0 miles   2,480 miles

ANTARCTICA

Index

snowline 30
snowmobile 49
snowy owl 56
soil 28 38 56 58
solar panels 11 55
Solar System 6-7
source (of a river) 26
South America 46 60
southern hemisphere 14 15
South Pole 14 48
space 5 6-7 10 11 34
spacecraft 4 7 8 9 10
space shuttle 11
space stations 10 11
spacesuits 8
spring 14 15
stacks 33
stalactites 40
stalagmites 40
stars 6 7
stepping stones 26
stoat 56
storms 18-19 28
streams 26 51
stumps 33
submarines 35
summer 14 15 17 29
Sun 6 12 13 14 15 16 17 42 55

sunlight 11 13 15 17
sunrise 12
sunset 12
supermarket 53

telescopes 7
termites 44
thunder 18
thunderstorms 17
tide 32 33
tigers 59
tornado 18
total eclipse 13
toucans 47
tourists 44 45 48 49
treasure 35 39
treeline 30
trees 19 22 30 38 44 46 47 55 57
  acacia 44
  baobab 44
  conifer 30
tributaries 26
trilobite 21
tunnels 39
turbines 55
underground 38-39 40
underground trains 39
USA 10 12 45 53 59

valley 26 36 51
Venice 53
volcanoes 20 24-25 28 36
  in sea 24 36
vultures 45

walkers 30
warthogs 45 57
water 16 17 40 42 51 54 55 58 59
waterfalls 26 27 40
water pipes 39
waves 19 28 32 33
weather 16-17 60
weaver birds 44
web of life 56-57
whales 35 48
  humpback 35 48
  killer 48
  sperm 35
wildebeest 44
wind 16 17 18-19 29 32 55
winter 14 15 29 31
wolf 56
wood 55
woodlouse 38
wool 55

Yellowstone National Park 59

Acknowledgements
The publishers are grateful to the following for permission to reproduce material:
p4 globe, Digital Vision; p9 Saturn 5, NASA; p10 Landsat, Digital Vision; hurricane, NASA Goddard Space
Flight Center; city, Digital Vision; sea temperatures, CLRC, Rutherford Appleton Laboratory; p11 shuttle,
CORBIS; p12 sunrise, Tony Stone Images/Tony Craddock; sunset, Digital Vision; p13 sun behind clouds, Tony Stone Images/John
Beatty; p16 sunflowers, Tony Stone Images/Tim Thompson; wind, Tony Stone Images/Art Wolfe; snow, Tony Stone
Images/Donovan Reese; p17 clouds (from Met. Office), R.D.Whyman; p18 tornado, Tony Stone Images/John Lund; lightning,
Digital Vision; hurricane, Will & Deni McIntyre/Science Photo Library; p24 volcano, Geoscience Picture Library; p27 waterfall,
Digital Vision; p29 Indian monsoon, Tony Stone Images/Martin Puddy; rice paddy, Tony Stone Images/Hugh Sitton; p31
avalanche, Tony Stone Images/Michael Townsend; avalanche hitting trees, Rex Features; rescue dog, Rex Features; p34 Pacific,
Tom Van Sant, Geosphere project/Planetary Visions/Sci Phot Lib; fishing boy, Julian Cotton Photo Library; trawler and net,
Tony Stone Images/Vince Streano; creels, Scottish Highland Photo Library/J Macphearson; p42 Africa, Tom Van Sant, Geosphere
project/Planetary Visions/Sci Phot Lib; p45 prairies, Tony Stone Images/Paul Stover; p46 South America, Tom Van Sant,
Geosphere project/Planetary Visions/Sci Phot Lib; p51 crevass, CORBIS; p53 Venice, Tony Stone Images/David H Endersbee; New
York, Tony Stone Images/Tom Hill; Jaipur, Tony Stone Images/Hilarie Kavanagh; p54 bottle bank, Tony Stone Images/David
Woodfall; p55 wind turbines, Tony Stone Images/A & L Sinibaldi; solar panels, Tony Stone Images/Bruce Hands; dam,
Tony Stone Images/Chris McCooey; p59 grizzly bears, Tony Stone Images/Kathy Bushue.

Every effort has been made to trace and acknowledge ownership of copyright. If any rights have been omitted, the publishers
offer to rectify this in any subsequent editions following notification.